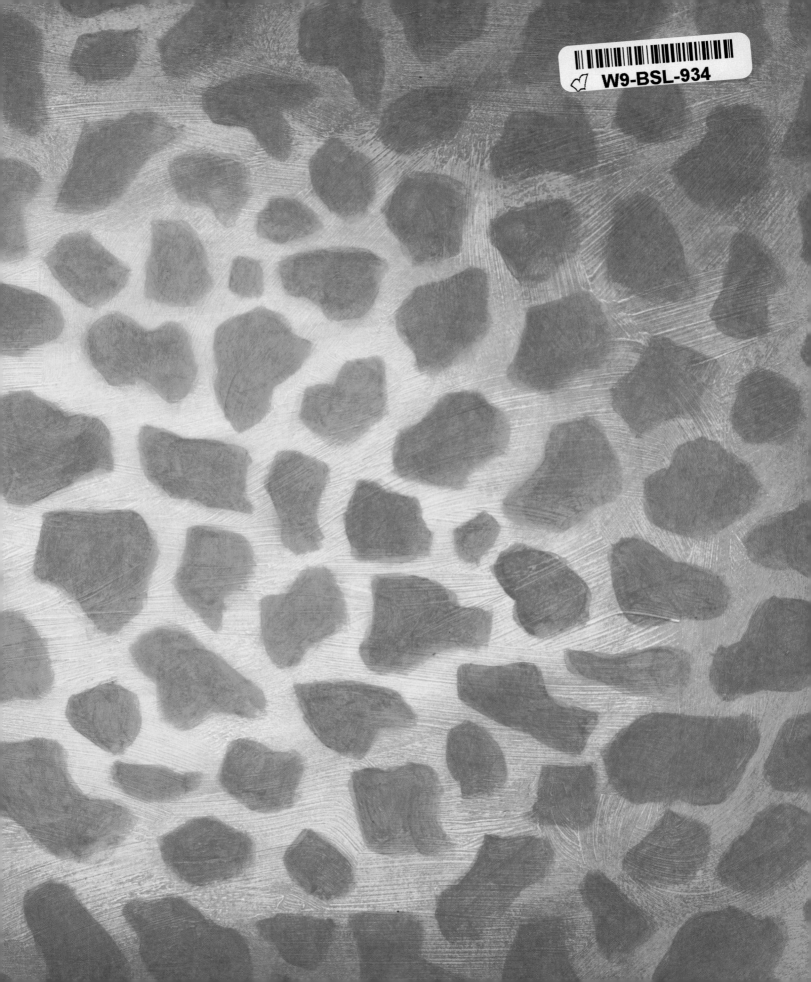

# Giraffe and Bird Together Again

## Rebecca Bender

pajamapress

**First published in Canada and the United States in 2018**

Text copyright © 2018 Rebecca Bender
Illustration copyright © 2018 Rebecca Bender
This edition copyright © 2018 Pajama Press Inc.

This is a first edition.

10 9 8 7 6 5 4 3 2 1

www.pajamapress.ca          info@pajamapress.ca

 Canada Council    Conseil des arts          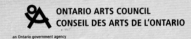 ONTARIO ARTS COUNCIL          Canadä
for the Arts      du Canada                   CONSEIL DES ARTS DE L'ONTARIO
                                   an Ontario government agency
                                   un organisme du gouvernement de l'Ontario

The publisher gratefully acknowledges the support of the Canada Council for the Arts and the Ontario Arts Council for its publishing program. We acknowledge the financial support of the Government of Canada through the Canada Book Fund (CBF) for our publishing activities.

**Library and Archives Canada Cataloguing in Publication**

Bender, Rebecca, author, illustrator
       Giraffe and Bird together again / [written and illustrated by] Rebecca Bender. -- First edition.
ISBN 978-1-77278-051-2 (hardcover)
       I. Title.  II. Title: Together again.
PS8603.E5562G575 2018          jC813'.6          C2018-901763-5

**Publisher Cataloging-in-Publication Data (U.S.)**

Names: Bender, Rebecca, 1980-, author, illustrator.
Title: Giraffe and Bird Together Again / Rebecca Bender.
Description: Toronto, Ontario Canada : Pajama Press, 2018. | Summary: "Adventurous Bird loves to try new things and visit new places. His friend Giraffe prefers his safe routine. But when Bird disappears, Giraffe braves a long and difficult journey to save his friend" -- Provided by publisher.
Identifiers: ISBN 978-1-77278-051-2 (hardcover)
Subjects: LCSH: Giraffe – Juvenile fiction. | Birds – Juvenile fiction. | Friendship – Juvenile fiction. | BISAC: JUVENILE FICTION / Social Themes / Friendship. | JUVENILE FICTION / Social Themes / New Experience.
Classification: LCC PZ7.B464Gi |DDC [E] – dc23

Cover and book design—Rebecca Bender

Manufactured by QuaLibre Inc./Print Plus
Printed in China

Pajama Press Inc.
181 Carlaw Ave. Suite 251 Toronto, Ontario Canada, M4M 2S1

Distributed in Canada by UTP Distribution
5201 Dufferin Street Toronto, Ontario Canada, M3H 5T8

Distributed in the U.S. by Ingram Publisher Services
1 Ingram Blvd. La Vergne, TN 37086, USA

Giraffe
(*Giraffa*)

Bush baby
(*Galagidae*)

Original art created with
acrylic and colored pencil

Ibex
*(Capra ibex)*

Dark Forest

Craggy Mountains

Bird
*(Aves)*

Yucky Muck

Dusty Plain

To Robyn, Weston, Wally, Zach, and James,
for the adventures you'll have

When it comes to adventures, Giraffe would say, **no, thank you.** He's perfectly happy right where he is. Gaze, graze, swat flies. Repeat.

Bird, on the other hand, would say, sign me up.
He feels alive in new places. Glide, swoop, soar. Explore!

This shouldn't be a surprise.
Giraffe eats the same thing every day and
never gets tired of it.

But Bird seems to have an endless appetite
for new flavors.

Playing hide-and-seek, it's not hard to find Giraffe. He always hides in the same spot.

With Bird, there's no telling where you'll find him.

One morning, Giraffe notices breakfast is quite peaceful.

Where is Bird?

*He's probably just hunting for bugs, thinks Giraffe, chewing his greens.*

By afternoon, Giraffe starts to worry.

*What if something has* **happened** *to Bird?*

He decides to follow the feathers.

First, the feathers take Giraffe into
a dark forest. He has to watch his head.

Before long, Giraffe is tangled in vines.
*Adventures are for the birds*, he decides.
Time to turn back.

But what if Bird is in trouble?

With a loud snort, Giraffe shakes his head and wrestles the vines until he is free.

SNNffft PPPBBLLS

Next, the feathers lead Giraffe
up a craggy mountain.

Step after step,
Giraffe climbs.
His hooves slip
on the rocky slope
until he tumbles
backward.

But this is no time
to give up.

*What if Bird*
*needs* help?

Giraffe is determined. He leans forward, digs in his hooves, and stomps all the way to the top.

Pausing for breath, Giraffe looks out over the view.

A shiny something gleams in the dusty plain below, and he spots a small and beaky someone next to it.

# Bird *does* need him!

Quicker than he could swat a fly, Giraffe slides down the rocky slope on the other side of the peak.

There, in a daze, under a metal
sign, slumps Bird.

Relieved to see his friend, Bird wraps
his feathers around Giraffe.

Bird is so happy, he forgets to warn
Giraffe of the yucky muck nearby.
Giraffe is so happy, he doesn't notice
the picture on the shiny sign.

Suddenly, Giraffe and Bird have
a sinking feeling…

Bird hops to his feet and calls for **help.**

QUICKSAND!

TWEE-TWOO
TWEE
TW

Everyone knows not to struggle in quicksand, so they don't.

Giraffe sinks deeper and deeper, and starts to **despair**. This is why he doesn't like adventures.

Bird is **worried** too—when will help arrive?
He stays close to Giraffe and tries to distract him.

Giraffe recounts his **perilous** journey through the dark forest and over the craggy mountains. As he tells his story, a strange thing happens. He begins to feel **proud** of himself. He **stands taller** and **taller**.

Below the soft sand, he feels solid ground under his hooves. With all his might, Giraffe pushes through the yucky muck.

Bird cheers him on.

Finally out of the quicksand, Giraffe flops, utterly **exhausted.**

Bird can see his friend is **pooped** and ready to go home.

But Bird is still full of **pep**, and he has an idea—more vines!

Help arrives at last, and
Bird puts them to work.

Before long, it's time to go.

After all of his fearless feats,
Giraffe would **still** say that
adventures are for the birds.

And Bird would no doubt say,
yep, he's right.

But they make a deal.

Bird will **wander** a little less...

if Giraffe will **explore** a little more.

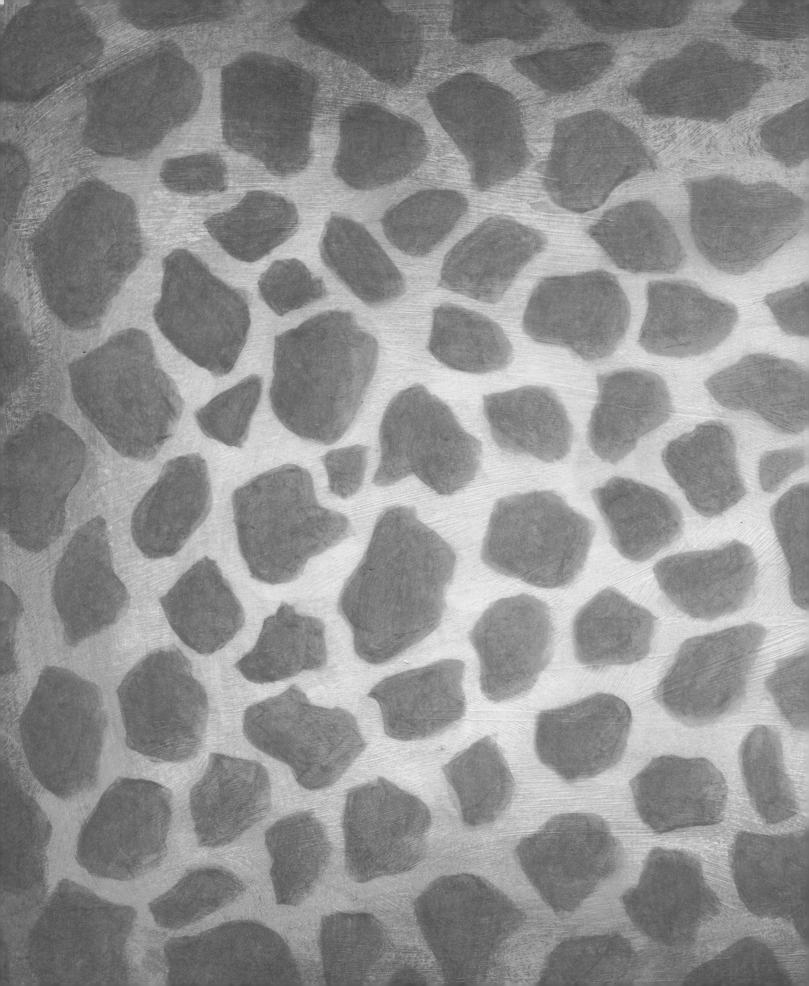